The Colors Inside Of Me

By Amy Lee Westervelt

Illustrated by Maddy Moore

Briley & Baxter Publications | Plymouth, Massachusetts

ISBN: 978-1-954819-22-1

Book Design: Stacy O'Halloran

Art class was Panda's favorite subject. He loved to take crayons back to his desk and create something beautiful. Sometimes the teacher would give the students materials and let them make whatever they felt inspired to create. Today, though, she gave them a special assignment.

"Class," she said. "Today I want you to draw a picture of yourself, and I want you to use all of the colors inside of you. Use your paper to show me the colors that make you who you are."

Panda looked at his paper and suddenly felt confused.

"I don't have any colors inside of me," he said quietly. "All I am is black and white. I don't know how to find the colors."

Panda looked up at the teacher and began to cry.

Meanwhile, the giraffe and the toucan were happily scribbling away on their papers, drawing spots and bright bold colors. They didn't have this problem. They were beautiful.

The teacher came over to Panda's desk, where he sat crying softly. "Panda," she began, kneeling down beside him, "you are a very kind student. You have a lot of great ideas, and you are a wonderful artist!"

"No, I don't have any color inside of me," said Panda. "Black is not a color and neither is white! I am boring!"

The teacher got up and went over to the bookshelf where she retrieved a book and brought it back to where Panda was sitting. He looked up as she opened it.

"Panda, this is a book about light. Did you know that all of the colors that exist are in the color black? And all of the colors are in the color white, too! You are full of potential! Let me show you!"

She turned to the first page, which was all blue.

"You have blue inside of you like the ocean! You have a calm gentle spirit. You help keep everyone peaceful and feeling safe," the teacher explained.

Panda stopped crying and fixed his eyes on her as she turned the page.

This page was bright red. Panda loved the way the color jumped off the page.

"Panda you also have red inside of you!" the teacher exclaimed. "You glow with passion when you are working on a project you love!"

"I have seen you spend an entire hour focused on a piece without ever looking up!" she continued. "You also get very passionate about sports! When you are playing soccer, you want your team to win! That is inside of YOU!"

She pointed to him playfully, and he giggled a little. He was starting to feel better.

The next page was yellow. Suddenly a little head peeked over the teacher's shoulder. It was the giraffe, who had heard Panda was upset. He came over to see what was wrong.

"Panda," said Giraffe, "you are my best friend! You are always there to help me when I need someone to talk to."

"You also are a great study buddy, and you make sure we keep on task while we are at school! You are happy and fun like the yellow sunshine!"

Giraffe reached out to hug Panda, who was so grateful for his friend. He was smiling big now.

The purple page was beautiful. The plum tones reminded Panda of the soft towels his mother kept in the bathroom. They smelled of lavender. He closed his eyes and thought of that smell.

Just then, Toucan flew over and landed on the other side of Panda. She was holding a purple crayon, which she proudly thrust into the air.

"Panda you are a loyal friend!" Toucan cried. "You always stick up for me on the schoolbus when the big animals are mean."

"You let me have the last chocolate milk at snack even though it is your favorite, and you always help me zipper my jacket when we go out for recess!" She smiled at him as she gave him a high five!

By this time, all of the classroom animals were beginning to gather to tell Panda how truly colorful he was. They lined up one by one to claim a page of the teacher's book.

You are amazing in the garden!

You always tell the truth!

When the book was done, all of the students were clamoring to tell Panda something they loved about him. He finally began to understand what the teacher meant about the colors inside of him.

CREATE

Every color that ever existed was inside of him! Maybe not all at once, but at some time, and they all made up who he was as a unique being!

As the teacher redirected the class back to the assignment, Panda felt his heart swell with pride. He raced up to the table and grabbed a box of crayons. Then he returned to his seat.

He took out the black crayon and began to draw his face. Then he filled in the details with the white crayon.

He sat back and looked at the panda on his paper and next he drew two hands and...

A giant rainbow!

The teacher walked around to see everyone's drawings and stopped by Panda's desk. She smiled. She knelt down and whispered to him, "Panda, you are an amazing, incredible being, and you can be, do, and have anything you desire in this world. I hope you see now just how much potential you have inside of you!"

Panda smiled back at the teacher. He knew she was right. He knew he was a wonderful manifestation of creation and that he could be anything he dreamed of becoming! All he had to do was close his eyes and imagine it.

And so he did.

Acknowledgements

This book is dedicated to the pieces of my heart: my husband and soulmate William and my children Alannah, William, Evainne, Caleb and Omri. You are the magic in my life!

Gratitude also goes out to my beautiful mom for believing in me and my dreams, my life coach Christine Rose Elle who helped me step into my intuitive power, and to my soul fam… you know who you are.

CPSIA information can be obtained
at www.ICGtesting.com
Printed in the USA
LVRC091039100821
695003LV00010B/344

* 9 7 8 1 9 5 4 8 1 9 2 2 1 *